Alison Bellringer

ESCAPE

AUSTIN MACAULEY PUBLISHERS®

LONDON * CAMBRIDGE * NEW YORK * SHARJAH

A CIP catalogue record for this title is available from the British Library.

ISBN 9781035873708 (Paperback)
ISBN 9781035873715 (ePub e-book)

www.austinmacauley.com

First Published 2024
Austin Macauley Publishers Ltd®
1 Canada Square
Canary Wharf
London
E14 5AA

By the Same Author

My Dog, Moss
Surprise at the Beach
The Bronson Escapades
The Wolf Cub
Whisper (Book One)
Lucas (Book Two)

Chapter One

"That's really not a good idea, Kaylee!" Pa said firmly, almost glaring at me for even daring to bring it up.

"I promised him, Pa," I objected immediately. "Carlos asked me days ago. And I already said that I would marry him."

"And I'm telling you it's not a wise thing to do," Pa replied angrily.

"What then? You'd have me break my promise?" My nostrils flared. "I thought you had brought me up better than that…"

"You know that's not what I meant at all," Pa grimaced. "I'm asking you to wait. Think about all the consequences your marriage will involve; then decide."

"We have decided!" I jutted out my chin. Ma and Pa would probably think I was being obstinate and downright stubborn. But really, I was just trying hard not to burst into tears of frustration. *Why won't Pa listen to me?* Even Ma seemed to be agreeing with him… "Carlos and I love each other – we are getting married."

"Seth, dear," Ma intervened, stopping Pa from making another sharp retort. "Perhaps we should discuss this another time… it's clear we all need to cool off and clear our heads."

She had been watching our exchange with a worried expression and merely wanted to smooth things over before they could get any worse.

Pa clenched his jaw even tighter at her request, but didn't say anything else: it was apparent that he thought there wasn't even anything more to discuss on the subject anyway.

"I told you we're getting married," I repeated firmly, as if to reinforce the statement. "You can't stop us."

"And I told you what my opinion on that is," Pa answered, barely managing to control himself. There was a fiery glint in his eyes as he struggled (with extreme effort) to speak calmly and in a moderate manner. "You are young, Kaylee. Barely sixteen. I'm just trying to advise you on such an important matter. You know that I want what's best for you to be happy. I'm only saying all this because I really don't want you to do something you might regret later on – there'll be no going back once you're married."

"Regret marrying Carlos?" My eyes widened in shock, unsure exactly what he was getting at. "There's no possible way that would ever happen!"

"At least think about it carefully first, Kaylee," Ma spoke up again, gently patting me on the arm reassuringly. "Take your time. No one is going to rush you into making such a decision before you're ready."

I am ready! I thought defiantly, emerald-green eyes flickering between the two of them. *But they are just trying to help... in their own way.* Ma's voice was kind, but I suddenly found her touch oddly disturbing rather than comforting. *I don't usually feel like that...* I normally welcomed her judgements on such vital issues. So why was I resenting their input now?

"Fine," I said aloud, eager to vacate the kitchen where I had so foolishly chosen to confront Pa about the candid plan to marry my sweetheart. "I will think about it. But that's not going to change anything – I do want to marry Carlos!"

Quickly, I turned and stalked away before either of them could say anything else. I headed straight towards my bedroom, wanting time to be alone. *They're probably expecting me to slam the door…* the thought crossed my mind as I entered the small space. So (purely out of spite), I refused to do so and forced myself to close it as quietly as possible. Then I threw myself across the bed and wept, burying my face deeply into the fluffy pillow to muffle the sound. *What should I tell Carlos?* I couldn't bear to see his face when he found out that Ma and Pa had refused their blessing. It would crush him! But what other choice did I have? I was too distressed and worn-out to think of anything. The argument with Pa had taken more out of me than I had originally thought – I was utterly exhausted. Then I remembered something even more concerning: I was supposed to be meeting up with Carlos again that evening. I had casually told him that I'd let him know what Ma and Pa had said, not expecting there to be any problem with it one way or the other. *Why are they making such a fuss?* I wondered. I really thought they had liked Carlos. *And it's not as if we hardly know each other or something, because we grew up together in the village, side by side.* We used to do everything together! Surely it was perfectly natural for us to want to take the next step and get married… A lump formed in my throat, and I tried to push each unnerving thought out of my mind. But it didn't work; I was still a bundle of nerves when I put on my coat and bonnet to go off and meet Carlos. *At least this conversation can't get any worse than the one with Pa earlier!* But it could. And I knew it too. I'd been around Carlos long enough to know that he would probably take the news rather badly (even worse than I had). I envied Ma and Pa somewhat – existing as an adult was far less difficult than still being an awkward, gangly teenager, with far fewer problems to deal with. Or so I imagined.

◆ ◆ ◆ ◆ ◆ ◆ ◆

I quickened my pace, hastening my steps to the place near the village green where Carlos had suggested we meet. We didn't have time to visit our favourite spot today: by the creek running almost directly behind Pa's property, where we lived in a particularly modest little cottage. I was completely out of breath by the time I got to where Carlos was waiting. A broad grin spread over his face when he saw me coming, and he stepped out from underneath the tall oak tree and enveloped me in a tight hug.

"Oh, Carlos," I clung to him for a moment. "It was awful! Just awful."

"What was?" Carlos moved slightly backwards in concern, surprised.

I hurriedly informed him of all that Pa had said, longing for the distasteful words to be out of my mouth. They had a bitter feel as each passed against my tongue. I glanced up at the young man standing before me, then looked away before he could make eye contact. Carlos stood silently, eyebrows furrowed in thought, listening intently as I spoke. When I had finally run out of words and apologies, all I could do was wait for him to speak. To react. And apparently, he was in no rush to do so. *This is it. He's going to tell me the engagement is off and there won't even be a wedding for us anymore. Any minute now, Carlos is going to break things off with me and walk away forever...* Carlos opened his mouth, forming the words, and I tried not to shuffle my feet in agitation.

"Well. That's not so bad, is it?" He said, almost too cheerfully. "They're not totally set against it, at least."

I jerked my head up from where I had been unobtrusively studying the ground and stared at him in disbelief. *What did he just say?*

"You're not..." I began, but was unable to continue. I had skipped dinner (refusing to leave the safe confines of my bedroom) and now my stomach was growling with hunger, distracting me.

"Not what?" Carlos searched my eyes questioningly. "I'm not what?"

"You're not angry with me?" I hesitated again. "You aren't considering terminating our engagement? It's not like it was completely official yet or anything..."

Carlos seemed to do a kind of double-take, and then he laughed. He laughed! I blushed at his response which indicated a serious lack of feeling. *How stupid and desperate had that question sounded...?* But Carlos' next words instantly put me at ease.

"Of course not!" He grabbed hold of my hands. "I love you, Kaylee. And I definitely still want to marry you – I'm certainly not about to withdraw my offer. What does it matter if we have to wait: we belong together. After all, where would I be without my golden-haired beauty?"

I smiled at his good-natured teasing. My long hair was really a dull brown, but according to Carlos, sometimes it shone brightly whenever it caught the sunshine at just the right angle. And as we exchanged pleasantries, I knew there was nothing in the world that I wanted more, than to be his 'golden-haired beauty'.

Chapter Two

I didn't broach the topic again with Ma or Pa, and they didn't mention it to me either. It was nearly a full week later, and I thought the whole thing had blown over. For some reason, I had convinced myself that Carlos and I were both content to wait upon our marriage (even though he hadn't actually specified how long of an interval that might entail). He seemed happy enough though, although a little more self-absorbed than usual. Carlos was normally pretty relaxed and care-free about everything, taking on board most things around him in a leisurely stride. He was in his late teens, so only a couple of years older than me. But I looked up to him greatly, like those extra few years had gained him much more wisdom than I had learned so far. I carelessly figured (with quite a lot of ignorance thrown into the mix) that Carlos had spoken independently to Pa and the alliance was sanctioned for some later date.

With all that being the case, I was quite startled when one day Carlos said he'd come up with a new plan for our immediate future and would I please meet him by the creek. I knew right where he meant; there was quite a decent-sized log on the bank where we often went to chat (the rather large piece of driftwood having been washed up onshore after a furious storm the previous winter). So I headed in that direction, wondering what it could be that he so urgently wanted to tell me. *Has Carlos somehow managed to convince Pa that it's okay for us to get married sometime this year, after all? And could he have changed Pa's mind about it so quickly?* I shook my head 'no'. It must be something else. Pa would not have given in so easily on that point (not when he was absolutely convinced that he was in the right). And nothing would be able to persuade him to think differently. *So what could Carlos possibly be referring to, that would cause such a strange disturbance to his otherwise normally placid manner?*

Carlos was so animated and spoke so fast, laying out his idea, that I could barely understand what he was even saying most of the time. I struggled to grasp it all. The very notion seemed totally incomprehensible – it had never even entered my mind as a potential possibility.

"You want to do what?" I blinked rapidly, trying to focus on his words once more. "The Reverend won't perform the ceremony for us, Carlos. He's one of Pa's closest friends and he will know that we don't have the proper permission. Anyway, Pa would never allow it."

"Then we'll just have to go somewhere else," Carlos wasn't about to be dissuaded from his course. "Find someone who will. Even if we have to head to another village to do it. Your pa doesn't have to know… not till after."

"You mean run away?" I gasped, shifting somewhat sideways on the log (I needed more space to process what was happening). *Does he really want to do that?*

"We wouldn't be running away," Carlos refuted emphatically. "We're just going to get married, then we can come back here. It's not like we're never going to return home. But we're not children anymore – why can't we decide what we should do? I won't be dictated to by our parents! After all, who better than us to sort out what we feel or how we should live… If we're going to get married, then why not now? Why waste time when we both already know what we want?"

"But…" My mind was scrambling to make sense of all this. "To go without Pa's blessing? There wouldn't be a real wedding you know, just some stranger pronouncing us 'man and wife'. And who will witness the right documents for us if no one else can attend?"

"It's not like he forbade us or anything," Carlos said (and there was some vehemence behind his words that I had never heard from him before). "Your pa just gave us some advice, so can't we work out for ourselves whether or not to heed it? What difference is it going to make if we go now or in a couple of years? We wouldn't really be disobeying, as he didn't actually give us a strict order that we agreed to abide by."

"Well…" As I thought more about Carlos' points, I could see that they were technically true (so in theory, he was right). But I knew it would greatly upset Ma if we were to follow through with such a thing. And all our friends in the village would completely miss out on a beautiful wedding! Something that was cherished by all, and held such delight for all the folks (young and old) whenever such an occasion was in the offing. "Perhaps we should consider this for a bit longer? There would be much to accomplish before making such a journey."

"Come on, Kaylee," Carlos droned on (almost moaning with impatience). "Just think about the looks on everyone's faces when we stride back into the village hand-in-hand as a married couple. It would be so worth it for that alone!"

"I must have time to think first," I paused, not wanting to put him off, but also not quite ready to fully commit to the plan. At least, not before I'd had a chance to reflect upon it all. "Really, Carlos. This is just so sudden."

"Very well," Carlos stood up, pursing his lips bitterly. He clearly wasn't at all happy about how it had gone over with me. "Think about it, if you have to. But remember, I can't wait forever."

He was practically scowling at me now and I should have noted the warning – there was too much haste. Carlos was being uncharacteristically impulsive, wanting to rush ahead, that for once he wasn't really listening. He certainly needed more time to develop in certain ways before settling down with a wife (I may have been willing to marry, but Carlos wasn't yet ready for the event). And besides, he'd already got the idea into his head and nothing was likely to stay his mind now, not until the deed was done. But none of that even entered into my consideration.

"Oh! I'm not having second thoughts about marrying you." I interjected sharply; fearful he had taken my hesitation the wrong way. "I really do! It's just that… well, there's so many implications. I don't know what to do…"

"I do," Carlos contested gruffly. He whacked his hat against his trousers, dislodging several clumps of dust, but stopped before wandering off. "Tell me as soon as you're ready then. And don't breathe a word to anyone else about this!" He cautioned as a final resort.

"Not even Monica?" I asked (though I knew what his answer would be).

"Especially not Monica!" Carlos snorted. "She's a total gossip. If you told her what we're planning, then the whole village would know by morning!"

I nodded, but my eyes were tearing up. I gathered that this was a burden I'd have to bear on my own. Monica Cordwell was my closest confidante and the only girl my own age who lived nearby. Despite my bias, even I could see that she loved to talk and nearly no secret would be entirely safe with her. Especially not one such as this…

"We can't risk anyone finding out, you understand?" Carlos continued, squeezing my hand in recompense. "They would merely try to stop us…"

I nodded again. My stomach was still churning from the unexpected revelation, but deep down, I knew my heart had already made the decision – we would be running away. *But how long did I have left?* How much longer with Ma and Pa before I'd cave in and say 'yes' to Carlos once again?

Chapter Three

Carlos lost no time in setting the date for our departure (he did so as soon as I'd given him my agreement). It was to be over the following weekend – only four days away. Four days to consider what items to bring along and what else we would simply have to leave behind. And four days to pretend everything was absolutely fine when it was far from it. My relationships with Ma and Pa seemed strained, constantly having to hide my preparations so that they would not get wind of anything untoward. They appeared their usual selves, unaware of how quickly their lives would change following my absence.

Neither Carlos nor I were particularly inclined to delay the night of our leaving now that we were both fully committed to seeing it through. It was decided that each of us would have to sneak out after dark (once everyone else was asleep). We had come to the rapid conclusion that we would simply have to walk the distance to whatever village we happened to come across first as we would not go so far as to 'borrow' someone else's horse or wagon which would be easily missed. So we had to limit the number of our belongings to what we could comfortably carry (which wasn't much). I wasn't too worried about that though. After all, we would soon be back and then able to collect the rest of our things from home. I was not expecting to be gone long – a week at most – so the thought of truly missing my friends and family did not really hit me until much later on (when our plans once again changed rather abruptly).

I nearly let it slip to Monica though, about our marriage intentions. It was the last day before we were to head off and I had been visiting the Cordwell's in order to have tea with my friend. That was to be the last such occasion for many years (although I had no way of knowing that beforehand, otherwise taking my leave of her would have been far more heartfelt than it really was).

"Take care of Ma, won't you?" I had asked glibly, momentarily forgetting that she didn't know about my great expectation to soon depart the area. "When I'm not here. She'll need company."

Well… Monica fixed me with such a stare from her intense pale-blue eyes, that I had to mentally backtrack to work out what I had said that should be so startling for her to hear.

"I mean, she likes it when you and your ma visit regularly." I quickly tried to cover up my blunder, but it was too late. Monica had obviously caught on to my mistake at once and would not stop questioning me to get to the bottom of whatever it was. If there was something amiss going on, then she just had to know!

"What do you mean, when you're not here?" The tall blonde tried coaxing for more information. "Why wouldn't you be here?"

"Oh, it's nothing," I shrugged, trying to remain casual. "Pa's got so many chores to do in the workshop, that she gets lonely when I'm off helping him. That's all."

Monica narrowed her eyes at me, clearly not convinced by this, but I remained indifferent and refused to let her get to me. I would have to watch my tongue more carefully for the rest of the day though. I swiftly made my escape from my friend's cottage (before I said anything else dubious), scurrying home to check yet again that everything was ready for later that night. *Only a few hours to go...* I thought, glancing at the sun's rapid progress across the bright blue sky. *Just one or two more days before Carlos and I will be legally married!* I almost gave a little skip, hardly able to contain so much excitement. How did the days pass so slowly, and yet so fast, at the same time?

◆ ◆ ◆ ◆ ◆ ◆ ◆

I had the bundle of things that I wanted to take waiting on my side dresser (consisting of a spare frock and other womanly necessities) which were efficiently wrapped in a warm blanket, with several handholds built in so that it would be easier to carry while we were on the move. I had to keep everything in my bedroom or else Ma would wonder what was happening! I just hoped she didn't wander into my bedroom unannounced, see there was no longer a cover on my bed, and realise that something extremely odd was going on (I couldn't exactly ask Ma for a fresh blanket to take along; she was pretty shrewd and would immediately become suspicious). I had no carry-case, and I couldn't think of anything else that would work to keep all the little bits and pieces together without checking with someone… As it was, I was a little surprised (and relieved) that neither she nor Pa had asked how it was all going with Carlos. While I couldn't exactly tell them the truth, I was sincerely grateful that I'd had no occasion to lie either. I don't think I could have anyway – it would all have come pouring out at even the slightest of nudges, and then that would be that. But everything seemed to be falling into place even better than I could have anticipated.

I did a few extra chores that evening. Partly to keep myself occupied, and partly so that I would have an excuse to be constantly hanging around the yard. I topped up the wood box with extra kindling, filled the kitchen bucket to the brim with fresh water from the nearby pump, and repeatedly swept along the porch. All the while keeping an eye out for Carlos. And finally, he came past, nodding towards me before continuing on. It was our agreed-upon signal – all our plans were now in place. We would be leaving that night, under the cover of darkness. The sky had clouded over so not even the moon would be there to light our way, but that just meant there was even less chance for someone to see us and risk getting caught. My thoughts turned grim as I tried in vain to cleanse my grubby hands, irrationally wiping them against an equally soiled apron.

There was just one thing left to do (and quite possibly the hardest). Write a short note of explanation to Ma and Pa for when they would be unable to find me at first light the next day. *Small comfort that would be…* but I had to say something so that they wouldn't worry. Well, not too much anyway. I knew they'd probably agonise over it right up until the time we returned. But it might at least deter them from sending a search party out after us or something like that.

Chapter Four

I fretted over the whole note-writing business for some time, scrunching up attempt after attempt, before deciding to settle for something simple and to the point (I hoped it didn't sound quite as brash or thoughtless in the reading, as it did when penning the words).

Dear Ma and Pa,

Please do not be concerned if you cannot find me tomorrow – I am going away with Carlos so that we can marry. We will soon return. I do not wish to cause harm but feel I must go with him, for our love cannot be broken, nor delayed. Your input has been valuable, though we must be able to choose our own path.

Your loving daughter, Kaylee.

I absolutely refused to read it over again and immediately stuck it on the dresser upon its completion, propped against the mirror where it would be easily seen. And when Ma was not looking, I quickly tossed the waded-up notes (those I'd deemed full of errors or not quite right for some reason) into the fireplace where they would burn and crumble into non-existence. It would not do to have Ma read one of those messages by accident instead of the one I'd intended for her to see! I thought it quite likely that Ma would be the one to spot it when she bustled in to wake me up and found nought but the pillow still on the bed. But I was pretty sure she would not read it properly until Pa had come back into the cottage for breakfast, after his early morning chores (on most days he was always the quickest one out of bed).

That evening, Ma and Pa fell asleep sooner than I expected. I had retired for the night first, but had forced myself to stay awake until no further sounds were heard coming from the other areas of the cottage. I could tell when all the candles had been snuffed out because no more light came filtering under their closed bedroom door leading out into the hallway.

"Goodnight, Ma," I'd given each of them a hug (feigning cheerfulness), before vacating the main living area somewhat earlier on. "Goodnight, Pa."

"What's up with her?" I overheard Ma asking as I disappeared around the corner. "Kaylee isn't normally such a hugger at this time of night – she's usually stuck in the middle of one of her teenage 'I'm tired, life isn't fair' tirades. Actually, Kaylee's been so moody lately I fear there's something seriously wrong with her."

"I wouldn't know about that," Pa chuckled back. "Perhaps she is slowly growing out of that and we'll soon have our happy Kaylee back again. I must admit that I've missed our little girl very much…"

I didn't catch Pa's response. If I had, I'm sure my heart would have contracted sharply at the offhand remark and swiftly been broken apart by those few simple words.

♦ ♦ ♦ ♦ ♦ ♦ ♦

It was time to go – I shouldered my pack and paused in the bedroom doorway, mentally surveying the room. Nothing was out of place: it was just as tidy as always. Only the empty bed and carefully scribbled note indicated anything out of the ordinary. Easy signs that the new day would bring something remarkably different (for all of us). I crept along the hallway as quietly as I could, trying not to bump into anything in the shadows that would waken Ma or Pa. I slunk out the front door and closed it behind me with a light clicking sound. Carlos was standing in wait by the gate, alert for any movement, expecting me to join him at any moment. Silently, I reached out my hand and he took it firmly before leading me out along the road (and away from everything I had ever known).

"Where are we going to go?" I whispered, as soon as I felt we were far enough away from the village to talk and not disturb anyone.

"The nearest village," Carlos whispered back straight away. "It shouldn't take us more than an hour or so to walk there."

"But won't people ask questions, Carlos?" I checked, suddenly feeling butterflies in the pit of my stomach. "Pa goes there for work sometimes, remember? Filling extra orders with his carpentry business."

"That's true. I had forgotten…" Carlos stopped in his tracks.

"I'm afraid we will have to go much further than that before no one will recognise us or casually report back that strangers were in town," I mentioned hesitantly. *Had Carlos already thought through that drawback himself?*

"You're right," Carlos hissed fiercely, obviously annoyed for not having thought of that particular problem earlier. "We'll just have to skirt around a few villages first."

I nodded. Then stupidly realised that it was so dark outside that he probably wouldn't have noticed my nearly imperceptible agreement at all. Carlos was probably still waiting for me to say something in response.

"That sounds sensible," I added, swiftly confirming my eagerness to go on.

"Let's keep moving then," Carlos replied easily. "We've got a long way to go before dawn arrives, if that's what we're going to do."

I could barely make out any of Carlos' tell-tale features: his sandy-brown curly hair, his small smattering of freckles, or even his clean-shaven chin. He was just a dark silhouette standing beside me (even darker than the ones caused by all the trees and undergrowth nearby). But I could still feel his smile – it travelled all through his body and then overflowed into mine as if we were mere extensions of the other.

Chapter Five

My feet were aching and I was limping slightly by the time we got to a place Carlos deemed suitable for our purposes and no one would be able to recognise us. We had been walking for most of the night, so the blisters (and lack of sleep) had made me rather weary. Even though I had worn my walking shoes, I much preferred going about barefoot and hadn't realised how unused to them I had become over the recent summer months. Actually, we were both rubbing our eyes and hiding yawns as we approached the centre of the village. The sun had already risen and the market area was busy with people coming and going about their daily tasks. Carlos stopped someone to ask where a minister might be found and we were quickly directed towards the small chapel down a narrow side alley.

We were soon met by a young, newly qualified minister and we spent the next few minutes simply admiring the elegant characteristics of the architecture in the building. After the minister had politely welcomed his unexpected visitors, the following conversation was uncomfortable at best.

"You're a little young to be getting married, aren't you?" Reverend Morris raised an eyebrow when we eventually presented him with our somewhat unusual request. I tried to hide a rude snort by coughing slightly – the man hardly looked any older than Carlos and he was already married. At least, he was if the fashionable young woman hovering by his elbow (who had introduced herself as the minister's wife) was to be believed. "Where are your parents?"

I stuttered a little, unsure how to respond as to the delicate nature of the question. But Carlos showed no such reluctance and managed to reply with an even tone, despite not having prepared an answer beforehand.

"They live quite a way from here." He claimed with no preamble (and rather truthfully). "Unfortunately, circumstances do not permit for them to attend."

I don't know whether Reverend Morris entirely believed us or not, but he agreed to perform the necessary formalities and further arrangements were quickly made. He seemed tense though, too young to know quite how to handle the situation (quite likely never having done such a thing before). We were just relieved the minister hadn't pried too much into our affairs and realised why we had even come to him in the first place. I would much rather have been wed at home, by our own dear Reverend, but I knew why it wasn't possible. And I had accepted that as a vital part of the procedure.

Reverend Morris urged us to take some rooms for the night with an elderly couple who operated the village inn, while the rest of the preparations wcrc bcing made. Carlos had to rush off to the jewellers to get a wedding ring designed (a simple gold band was all that was required) while I dashed over to ask a neighbour who lived near there, if I could use a colourful bouquet of flowers from her garden. I had noticed the wide array of wild roses growing alongside the boundary fence earlier and then asked Reverend Morris' wife who owned them. I had seen them when we were first on the way over to the chapel and just loved them, pointing out my favourite to Carlos who also admired them briefly (but probably not quite as much as I did!).

It was hard to believe, but early the next morning, we were married. I wore an elegant, practical dress of navy blue which I had made by hand some time ago (unaware that it would eventually become my wedding gown). Carlos had on a simple suit with a black waistcoat and bowtie. We exchanged short vows, and in a matter of minutes, it was over and we were thanking the minister and his wife for officiating and signing our certificate of marriage. And then we were walking out the chapel doors, wondering what was next. *Did anyone ever really know?*

❖ ❖ ❖ ❖ ❖ ❖ ❖

"Are we going home now?" I asked when we paused on the sidewalk, deep in contemplation.

I think we both felt a bit lost – our only objective being fulfilled so suddenly like that. Maybe Carlos had expected everything to take longer, for he had given me the decided impression that we would be gone for several days (perhaps even a whole week!) before returning to our much-loved village; where I hoped Ma and Pa would be eagerly awaiting us with open arms. But that was not to be the case at all.

"Not yet," Carlos shrugged dismissively. "Let's not go back there for a while, give them time for everything to simmer down before our impromptu return."

"What are we going to do then?" I tried to brush aside a sharp pang of disappointment. "We have no money. No place to stay…"

"I'll just have to find work someplace," Carlos didn't seem too fazed by my comments.

He was a kind of apprentice handyman, so Carlos could probably get a job in any village he liked. And I had always wanted to explore more of the countryside than just what I could see from our own back yard, so we fleetingly resolved to travel around. Hurriedly, we picked up our things from the inn and bid the respectable couple farewell. Then we left the village. Further and further abroad we went. One week. Two weeks. Months stretched into a year, and still we could not quite bring ourselves to head home. I wanted to, on some days, but Carlos always put it off by saying it wasn't quite the right moment yet. I missed my old life at times, various events or memories often hitting me during the most mundane of activities. But overall, being married to my dearest Carlos was wonderful – I was living my dream.

Chapter Six

It was slow at first, but gradually, I saw Carlos begin to change. He was no longer the gentle, care-free young man I had chosen to marry. He was snappy and irritable, complaining about even the slightest mistake I had made in completing the variety of tasks around the space we lived. I had folded his clothes wrong or added the incorrect ingredient to his favourite soup… I was utterly confounded by it. Every word I spoke after being reprimanded only seemed to anger him further, and soon I took to hardly speaking at all (except whatever was necessary in order to follow his bidding). I could not fathom what had happened – I barely even knew Carlos anymore. I stayed with him out of duty and fulfilled my obligations as a wife, all the while wondering if Pa had been right and we should never have taken such drastic steps to run off when we were younger.

Recently, Carlos had taken on steady work at a dockyard situated near a large town. We rented a basic room at a boarding-house on the outskirts of the town so we would have lodgings, and sometimes he stayed with me, and other times not, depending on his workload (or mood). It was a rough environment for such an inexperienced man to be in and Carlos really had to put his back into it and grind his teeth in order to earn the approval of his fellow workers. But the pay was decent and soon Carlos had earned enough to purchase a tiny cottage in the woods, about half a day's walk from the town. The place was a bit rundown, but I managed to keep it reasonably clean and liveable. I usually enjoyed the solitude, but ofttimes it did get lonely, and then I sought solace in going for a daily walk amongst the trees. I quickly grew accustomed to every inch of the surrounding woods and its multitude of resident creatures.

It rapidly got to the stage when I never knew when to expect Carlos back each day. He regularly stayed out late with his 'workmates' and only his heavy boots thumping along the path would signal his return. Then I would have to rush to reset the table and make sure his dinner was appropriately heated through (and not grown too cold on the stove) before he had time to pick another fight with me about it not being done properly enough to his taste.

Whenever I was brave enough to mention going home, or at least a visit to Ma and Pa, Carlos seemed to get worse than ever and I quickly learned to hold my tongue. He had the audacity to forbid the event and clearly never wanted the topic to come up again. I knew he wasn't happy and that Carlos was not telling me much of what went on while he was absent every day, not that I really wanted the gruesome details (typical sailor talk wasn't particularly acceptable to most ladies). But even though he hardly spoke about his work, I gathered enough to assume that something there was making him uncomfortable and ashamed of how he was living. Carlos attempted to convince me that we were settled, that everything was fine and we had no reason to change locations or for him to search out other work. When asking him why we had to have a cottage in the middle of nowhere instead of having a house in the town itself (where it would be thoroughly more convenient for both of us), Carlos told me that he was sheltering me from that loathsome place. But how could he be, when he showed up at all hours of the day or night, completely drunk and hurling verbal insults around for something so trivial as me just standing in the wrong place? Did he really think that his incessant shouting was a good way of 'sheltering' his wife from anything detestable that should never so much as even taint her world?

If I had realised then how closely to Ma and Pa's village we had settled (roaming in a sort of criss-cross formation, like a large circuit, on our travels), I might have found some way to go back or at least send them some indication of where we were. But the constant journeying had disorientated me and the directions had quite thoroughly blurred in my mind. Even so, I might have covertly asked around in town to find out how to get in touch with them. I might have, were it not for the child I was carrying... Carlos' child. I clutched my stomach, feeling another jolt come pressing against my innards. I was terrified and rather apprehensive of what Carlos might do when he found out about his unplanned son or daughter. But I also had hope – hope that my real Carlos would come back to the surface upon the birth of our baby. That he would return to his usual considerate self and things would be again as they should have been right from the beginning. Would a daughter encourage his former fondness for helpless little ones? Or would he entirely dismiss the child as being weak and not even worth the bother of knowing?

◆ ◆ ◆ ◆ ◆ ◆ ◆

On a particularly bad day, I rushed away from the cottage in tears. I had just informed Carlos of my late pregnancy (after a long time avoiding the issue and intentionally skirting around the problem), and he only grunted in response. We were finally starting a family of our own, and he grunted…? I was so upset by his brusque casualness, that I could stay in the same room with him no longer.

Somehow (without being able to see), I managed to stumble my way to the stream where I usually fetched our drinking water from. I sank down beside a large boulder and wept. I cried for home. For Ma and Pa, and my friends. My failed marriage. Carlos. Our dreams and optimistic plans for the future that had come crashing down around us. And for our unborn baby… Would that child ever see the man I had once loved? And still did at heart. Or would they only see the horrible figure of who Carlos had turned into afterwards? *What's to become of us now? Who can I ask for help?* I didn't have the answers, just more and more questions. An endless number of problems that could not be fixed.

I don't know how long I lay there on the grass, but it felt like a long time. When I came around, I sat up and brushed stray clumps of dirt off my clothing before washing my face in the cold water of the stream. Once that was done, I felt fresher and carefully took a moment to look around. I hadn't come this far upstream before – I usually walked in the other direction, back towards the town. If I hadn't been so distressed earlier, I might have noticed how pleasant my surroundings were. I breathed in deeply, soaking in the calm atmosphere.

And then I heard a sound, like a plaintive whimper. I opened my eyes and tried to figure out where it was coming from and what animal was making the noise. It was certainly no bird, and not something I was at all familiar with (or expecting). I couldn't see anything unusual from my position so I stood up and walked towards where I thought it was coming from. Closer and closer I got, and the whimpering rose in volume and intensity. And then I saw it – a big, short-haired yellow dog. Soulful brown eyes stared mournfully at me as if asking for attention. One hind paw was tangled up in the underbrush and the dog looked exhausted in the attempt to pull free (like it had been stuck there for some time trying to get away). I mightn't be able to solve all of my problems, but I could certainly work on his.

As I spent the following few minutes freeing the dog's paw, I chatted to the friendly animal. The sweet creature waited patiently, even seeming to listen by flicking his ears back and forth and tilting his head slightly to one side. When I had pulled away the last branch and mess of leaves from around his paw, the dog bounced about in joy, gratefully licking my hand. I may have been worn down with thoughts of my own burdens previously, but in that moment, something happened to lift me out of my earlier despair. Just the simple way in which the poor dog seemed to be thanking me for taking the time to stop and help him out of his predicament went a long way towards making me feel better.

I wandered back over to the boulder and sat down on it, not quite ready to face Carlos again if he happened to still be in the cottage, waiting for me. Instead of taking off as I'd expected, the dog seemed to know instinctively that I required companionship for a while. Instead, he came and sat beside me with his heavy head resting on my lap (allowing me to stroke his soft, velvety ears). They were a darker shade of yellow than the rest of his body, more of a deep honey colour, nearly the same shade as the sweet substance we could purchase from the store back home. We stayed like that for quite some time, sitting quietly, just gaining strength from one another.

At last, I knew it was time to head back and wondered vaguely if the dog might choose to follow. But he didn't. The intelligent creature watched me leave with a sad, contemplative look on his face, before resigning himself to trotting off in the opposite direction.

I went back to that place several times in the next few weeks, but I never saw the special dog again. I did find a sort of cubby-hole though, near the spot where he had been caught in the bushes (just the right size for a small child to suitably hide in…). Even though I didn't see the dog, I remembered him fondly, and thereafter referred to him as 'Old Tangle' in my mind, whenever I thought back to our treasured meeting.

Chapter Seven

I sang numerous songs from my childhood that I remembered Ma humming to me when I was little, hoping one of them would help to settle Britney quickly back to sleep. She was a fussy baby, but that was probably partially just a result of how stressed and jumpy I was most of the time. But the frail young thing nearly always seemed more content when I was holding her in my arms and singing the lullabies for our pleasure. Only then did Britney seem truly happy and blink back up at me with a smile dimpling each cheek in turn. Those were my favourite moments of each day – when I would cuddle her close and hear her timid gurgling. But I was constantly afraid of what Carlos might do. I had named our daughter Britney because the moment my husband had first asked me to go out with him, he'd confessed he had always wanted a daughter with that name. The idea had stuck in my mind so much, that I couldn't think to call her anything else. And I so wanted it to connect the two of them even more deeply… although the first time I had introduced her to Carlos, he had merely shrugged in complete indifference.

Day by day, we struggled. And little Britney grew, yet remained slender and rather feeble. I did what I could but she was barely getting enough food just to hold on. I scrimped and saved but it did little good, and I could never afford to do anything about it. Britney even began to toddle about the floor and in the wee garden area I had erected, except she never strayed too far, lifting up her arms to me whenever she got too tired to go on. Then I would gather her up and I'd just talk to her while she sat listening on my knees. Always listening, never speaking. Britney was my only consolation in the trying few years following her difficult birth.

The first time Carlos hit me struck hard! The sound of the blow almost seemed to echo throughout the room. It was so startling and unlike him that I totally froze; my red cheek swelling up into a deep welt almost immediately. The instance even seemed to surprise Carlos: the fact that he had actually gone so far as to strike me with his bare hands. The moment was over with so swiftly, that I hadn't even time to react properly. Carlos was extremely quick to storm back outside, and after that episode spent even less and less time at the cottage with us. He never told me when he would be back, so I always had to be ready for him.

A new pattern ensued – eat, shout, slap, march off. Every night was more or less the same. I never cried in his presence, although silent tears would often run down my swollen cheeks unbidden afterwards. It was extraordinary how much they stung! But wiping them away only hurt the fragile spots even more. I knew it was only a matter of time before Carlos turned on Britney, so I always tried to deflect his attention elsewhere in order to protect her from his inexplicable fury – I could never quite tell when something random would set him off and his annoyance flare up indignantly for no particular reason.

"She's not here," I repeated matter-of-factly, whenever Carlos were to ask after the child (even though I knew perfectly well that it wasn't true and risked causing an even greater scene if he ever found out that I was lying to him).

Britney had rapidly taken to scurrying under the table and staying entirely out of sight whenever she heard Carlos coming. And I didn't blame her – I wanted to do much the same thing. But I couldn't risk him finding her. I just hoped Carlos' weighted work boots wouldn't bump into her by accident because he wasn't aware that she was underfoot. After Carlos had vanished down the path, I would coax Britney out and rock her close as she so frequently sobbed her little heart out.

"Whisper, Britney… Ma's here," I soothed, often simply crouching on the floor until we had both calmed down enough to expend the intense effort of rising again.

◆ ◆ ◆ ◆ ◆ ◆ ◆

Every few days I would need to walk into town to purchase fresh supplies and those times were especially frightening. I was too nervous to leave Britney alone in the cottage, and even though she was small, the child was still too heavy for me to carry all that way (as well as the full shopping basket on the return trip). And then I remembered the hidden gap in the bushes where I had found the distressed dog all that time ago. It would be a perfect place to pop Britney in whenever I had to leave her behind. Somehow (even without words), Britney seemed to know that she had to stay put. Even when I was away for several hours at a time, I always found her in pretty much the same spot: waiting. But I knew it was only a temporary solution at best, and began to consider what other precautions I could take to shield our daughter. *What would be best for Britney in the long run?*

Gradually, a plan began to develop, but it was so awful, so horrible to contemplate, that I kept pushing it aside. I was unsure if I would be strong enough (or even capable) of pulling it off.

Time passed, and before I knew it, I realised that somehow our little girl had turned five (although she was so tiny, that Britney could still be quite easily mistaken for being only three!). Birthdays had come and gone, along with other holidays, without either of us noticing – they had never been significantly different from other days to have warranted a celebration of any sort. And as I observed her, I saw that Britney lived in perpetual terror of her pa and I could delay the outlined strategy no longer – I had only one choice. One course of action to take. But how could I give up dear little Britney whom I loved with all of my being…? Perhaps it was not wise, but in that moment, I could think of no other way. I knew it would be the hardest thing I would ever have to do, but I feigned cheeriness anyway, determined that Carlos wouldn't know any different.

The dreaded day came, and the minute Carlos had taken himself off to work I began to get Britney ready. I wrapped her warmly in a blanket, which I'd previously cut armholes out of, and handed the child a small package of food to hold on to. I tried to talk normally while I was doing this, but my throat constricted too much to keep chattering endlessly on without knowing what to say (and I wanted to conserve what little strength I had). Britney seemed to know that something was quite gravely wrong, staring at me wide-eyed with her jaw almost gaping open, as she watched me bustling about. Then I put on my own cloak and picked her up, clinging tightly to Britney as I left the cottage.

I walked. And walked. And then kept right on walking. Britney grew heavy in my arms but I was reluctant to put her down, wanting to spare the child from the brisk pace I had set for myself. So I carried her, heading even further and further away from the only place she knew.

It was well into the afternoon before I finally stopped along the edge of the path and set Britney down. My arms were probably aching from her weight, but I barely noticed all that when my heart felt like it was being torn apart from the inside out. I kept glancing around furtively, almost expecting someone to be following us, but there was never anyone else in sight.

"Now, Britney," I knelt beside her and pointed my finger in the direction we had been going in. "You must continue walking. Keep going no matter what. Do you understand?"

Britney simply looked bewildered, but nodded anyway. I tried to brush aside tears that insisted upon pouring down my face (despite every intention of preventing them from coming). *How do you explain such things to a child? Why, oh why, must we be separated so!* I hugged her tightly for an all too short moment, then gazed into her eyes, wanting to remember them perfectly.

"Go, child." Even though everything within me cried out against it, I gave Britney a gentle nudge to get her moving again. "Don't look back."

I was glad she obeyed, for then she would not see how broken I had become. But Britney was still clearly confused that I was sending her away from me. I wanted to go with her… longed to be with her! To face the world together! I knew everything would be so new and unfamiliar to her. But I could not. Carlos would simply follow and nothing good would be achieved. But this way… maybe one of us would make it. Britney could find somewhere safe. Another family to take her in and provide a roof over her head. *And me? What will happen to me? Would Carlos notice her absence?* That was the only reason I would be staying – I would be going back to face his wrath alone.

Chapter Eight

I completely lost track of time after that – days felt like years, and years days. They all blurred into one another. I craved companionship with others but dreaded trips into town. Wrapped in my cloak and shawl, I tried to cover the bruises, but the aftereffects remained. I concocted my own salve to rub over them and yet they turned a dark shade of purple before they faded away, leaving ugly scars in their place. Some were worse than others but they each bore the mark, the memory of Carlos' extreme displeasure. The folks in town must have noticed, but they ignored the obvious in the apparent hope of avoiding awkward conversations (let alone confronting my husband with his mistreatment). Many women I saw were also facing similar things in their own homes, and had more children in tow, but were just as helpless to rectify the situation as I was.

One afternoon was unlike any other… Carlos' palm whacked into me so hard that I gasped aloud and stumbled backwards a few steps simply from the force of it. I think it was just as much out of habit by now as payment for anything I'd done. Even so, I completely lost my balance and hit my head against the firm, unyielding floor of the kitchen – it was the first time I had been rendered totally unconscious by one of his fits. I lay there (awkwardly sprawled out), unmoving, for a long time as the minutes ticked slowly away. Unbeknown to me, Carlos took off running from the abhorrent scene, in horror of what he had supposedly done.

When I eventually began to stir, my head throbbed! I sat up a little too quickly and instantly felt quite dizzy. Lifting my hand up to touch my forehead, I felt only blood. It was trickling down one side of my temple and there was a small pool of it near to where I had been lying. After gathering my wits, I cleaned up everything so that there was nothing left in the cottage to show what had occurred. Even the cut was hardly noticeable once the drops of blood had been washed away.

I pottered about, my mind clouded (hazy with a multitude of half-constructed thoughts), waiting for Carlos to return. But he didn't come. Several days went by, and yet he did not appear on the path – no footsteps thumping on the ground, no booming voice shouting to be heard, no orders, no nothing. Carlos was nowhere to be seen. *He's deserted me...* I thought, finally arriving at the logical conclusion. Gathering all of my courage together, I went to the dockyard to find him. But his manager snorted in contempt when I questioned him on Carlos' whereabouts.

"That rogue?" The man banged angrily on the nearby wall (it was just as well the makeshift shack was built strongly, or he would soon have found something to throw across the walkway, perhaps even unintentionally hitting an oblivious potential client looking to hire his services). "He hasn't shown up for work in days! It's like he completely disappeared or something. I should never have taken him on! Even the other men around here are wary of his current reputation and won't give me any information about him. That's if they do actually know anything, which I'm not convinced they do. And judging by your state, if I were you, I'd be glad he was gone…"

I was only too pleased to get out of there and go back to the cottage. *Well...* I thought, looking around the poorly furnished rooms. *There's nothing here for me now. I might as well pack up and try to find Britney, if I can. But will she know me at all? She was so young the last time we were together. Will I even recognise my own daughter?*

◆ ◆ ◆ ◆ ◆ ◆ ◆

I took everything useful that I could carry from the cottage and set off, following in Britney's footsteps so many years earlier. I drifted from village to village, one place then another, seeking reports if anyone knew of a small child travelling alone. But no one remembered a young person fitting the partial description I offered, fractured as it was. Each one of them smiled kindly back at me and shook their heads, sometimes giving me the option of staying in their homes for a while if I wanted to. And at times, it was such a relief to get a well-deserved rest, but always I pressed on within a few days, driven by the ultimate need to see Britney again. To know she was being well looked after and that I'd done the right thing by her. I just had no idea which direction to head in. *Where had she gone?* I didn't know.

I was nearing the end of my endurance by the time I made it to the right village. It should have looked remarkably familiar from such a close distance, but I was so weary (and it had all changed so much) that I did not. I stumbled and fell to my knees, unable to get up, and unaware of the fact that I had been to this village before – it had been my childhood home for years! But nothing about it registered. I felt faint. Someone called out, but my mind was so foggy I could not comprehend any of the words. Not until I felt strong, slender arms pulling me out of the grogginess did I lift up my face to mutely lock eyes with a beautiful child. A girl. With discerning bright blue eyes. Britney!

It took a moment, as time seemed to stand still, but she did know me… and then I heard her voice. Her true voice – my daughter was speaking to me! It was the most precious sound. We laughed and cried, overjoyed to be near our loved one again. And then Britney helped me walk steadily along the path, talking non-stop as she led me to the cottage where she lived with 'Grandma Ruby'. I was too focused on listening to her voice, that none of the actual words really sunk in. Otherwise I might have recognised everything at once – the pristine gate, the vegetable garden, the pump, the small porch, and the cottage itself. The elderly, grey-haired woman seated at the kitchen table… She rose and turned towards us as Britney tugged me further into the room. *That face. The way she held herself…* I paused, awed.

"Ma?" I asked, just as Britney had done only minutes before.

The old woman looked stunned, disbelief flickering through her eyes as she rushed forward to greet me with her arms outstretched.

"Kaylee?" Ma breathed sharply. "Kaylee – you're here. You've come back!"

Britney shrank behind me, obviously confused that we should know each other so intimately when she'd only just now introduced us. But I couldn't think about that. The only thing that was going through my mind was that after long last, I was finally being reunited with my own ma.

Chapter Nine

All of us had a lot to catch up on, years we had missed in the lives of the others, and we sat around the table taking turns to fill in the wide gaps of our tales and individual journeys. We talked, laughed, and cried in turn, adjusting our demeanour to suit the conversation in hand whenever the tone inside the cottage changed.

I was surprised to learn that not only had Ma been the one to take in my wayward daughter, but that I now had a step-brother as well. Apparently, Ma and Pa had hired the orphan boy soon after I'd run off and then ended up adopting him a short while later. Lucas was several years younger than me, and seemed just as astonished as I was. He was a thoughtful person, solid in build with a kind, teasing twinkle shining out of his eyes. I found myself trusting him almost immediately. Lucas had taken over from Pa as the village carpenter, filling the workshop with all sorts of cheer and goodwill. Pa… How I wept when I found out that he had passed away mere months after Carlos and I had fled.

"He was very sick," Ma comforted, insisting that I wasn't to blame in any way.

But there was so much to take in, so many scrambled thoughts rushing through my head, that I begged leave to go and rest.

"You take as long as you need, dear," Ma nodded wisely. "We're just so glad 'ta have you here again."

Britney had taken over my old room, and Lucas occupied the other. So for now, I simply stretched out on top of Ma and Pa's double bed and tried to relax. But I couldn't sleep. Whisper, Britney's black and tan shepherd, paced after and watched over me with intelligent dark eyes. How special it was (and even more meaningful), that my daughter had found the dog as a pup by the same spot where I'd met Old Tangle! The memories were buried deep within me, but I felt closer to my precious daughter than I ever had before.

◆ ◆ ◆ ◆ ◆ ◆ ◆

I started to help Britney with her daily chores and we cherished the time together, catching up on what had once been lost. I couldn't believe how much she had grown and often caught myself wondering how all this had come about (even though it had been explained to me over and over again!). Really, of all people, and it was my own ma that had provided her with a good home and stability with 'Uncle Lucas' as Britney liked to call him. All this time, and she was growing up alongside her own grandmother without even knowing!

Gradually, my inner strength began to return and I regained much of my youthful vigour (though I never forgot the life with Carlos and the love we had shared at the start of our relationship). I often wondered where he'd gone on that last day, but I was content to know that Carlos would never be able to hurt Britney in one of his drunken rages. I don't think he really knew what he was doing to us then, somewhat screened by a sort of moral blindness as to what his actions meant to those around him. Those who should have gained Carlos' care and protection, but instead only lived in fear of him. The people who should have mattered and desired his full consideration (especially towards the one who grieved the most for his deprivation – Carlos' own partner in marriage). It was at that moment, when simi-understanding came over me, that I realised I had forgiven him for my part. Truly forgiven Carlos for his many misdeeds. Henceforth only wishing him well, but still reconciling myself to the fact that the life we had envisioned together as a young married couple would never be.

Chapter Ten

Unfortunately, my good friend Monica Cordwell had moved away with her family and I was sorry not to see her around the village anymore. But I had other acquaintances living nearby and I could visit and have tea with the other women as I had once done. And there were lots of children about (friends of Britney, some of them were), and it seemed every person my age had married and parented several over the years. *I won't be having any more...* I mused, happy to be surrounded by eager youngsters again, but sorry that I could not add to their number. *Not without Carlos...* But Britney was thriving, and I couldn't get enough of the girl's lively chatter (the likes of which she seemed to have in abundance). The cottage was generally considered to be the same joyful home that I remembered it being.

And then the rumours started – some well-dressed man was eagerly searching for his missing wife and daughter! *Could it be?* We all had our doubts, but I tried hard to put on a brave face for Britney, masking my true feelings on the matter (who saw through the charade almost immediately). *But he couldn't be Carlos... the man had given the wrong name. Could somehow everyone be mistaken at the same time?* I tried not to give in to my wishful thinking, but it wasn't easy! On the contrary, it was always challenging and quite often difficult not to ponder repeatedly upon the notion, incredible as it was. *What if the strange man was Carlos? What if he'd seen the error of his ways and now wanted to make amends? What if he had come home begging for forgiveness?* There were too many questions. Too many unknowns. And I felt myself slowly withdrawing once more from the world around me.

◆ ◆ ◆ ◆ ◆ ◆ ◆

So much time passed when nothing further happened, that I dismissed the rumours and practically drew them completely from my mind. I had cast all thought of it aside until the day Britney burst through the cottage door in tears, screaming incoherent words. She was quickly followed by Lucas, who looked so worried that fear struck at my heart immediately.

"I saw him!" Britney whimpered, clinging to me and practically burying her face into the folds of my dress. "Pa's coming…"

This statement was met with a loud knock on the door (which thankfully Lucas chose to answer). But I recognised Carlos' voice even from that distance. I would have known it anywhere! And while Lucas chatted easily with him, I took Britney and hid at the other end of the cottage so that my husband would not see us. I wanted to be angry at Lucas for inviting him inside (after all, he knew what Carlos had done to us), but I couldn't. Not yet anyway. Common sense told me that Lucas had a good reason, and when he later explained, I did understand. Well, I understood enough to know he meant well, not that I totally approved of the way he had gone about it. Lucas had claimed that Carlos would be off sooner if he didn't find us, but he had not had enough time to think through the likely scenario that anyone in the village would probably be quite capable of pointing us out (or even recognising Carlos alone), which was a major flaw in his plan.

We didn't hear from Carlos again though, and ofttimes Britney caught me just standing in the yard, simply staring in the direction I thought he'd taken. She seemed puzzled by it, uncomprehending what I saw in it, but Britney didn't question me about it either. I knew we were still getting used to one another's habits, although it still felt odd that she didn't ask what I was thinking about at the time.

Chapter Eleven

Once, when it was my turn to fill up the bucket with fresh water from the pump, I placed my thickest shawl around my shoulders because the evenings were getting chilly. The sky was already darkening as I picked my way across the yard. And I heard the soft echoes of a familiar voice drifting in the air, floating towards me on the breeze. I turned quickly and saw the dark shadow of a man standing by the gate and I dropped the bucket with a sharp clang.

"Kaylee?" The figure said, and I knew it was real and not something I'd just imagined. "At last... I've been looking everywhere for you!"

"Carlos?" I shivered uncontrollably. "You left me..."

Carlos came several paces forward and I could see he looked pained. Even so, I stepped back to put more distance between us again and he stopped as if uncertain what to do next. There followed a tense conversation whereupon we both fired terse questions at one another, desperate for the other to hear what we had been through. *Ma? Please come outside, Ma... Can't anyone hear us arguing?* I wanted to listen to Carlos' apology, but I was too agitated to adhere to it. I was feeling uneasy being alone with him after what had happened the last time. *Won't someone come outside to investigate what's going on...?* Very soon I heard the cottage door slamming, but my relief was rather short-lived when I heard Britney's voice calling out to me – instantly all the pain came flooding back. The distraught sobbing. Forcing my daughter to live a life of constant hunger and dread. So I braced myself against Carlos' onslaught of explanatory words: I cowardly held myself aloof from his earnest begging.

"Ma?" Britney wandered over, unaware of her pa's presence. "What are you..."

She finally noticed who I was talking to and abruptly turned away, practically melting into my side.

"Tell him to leave, Ma," Britney mumbled. "I don't like it when he's here."

I couldn't answer, and merely watched the jaw-dropping revelation dawn on Carlos. It was clearly visible, the unexpected news flash travelling all over his face. My husband looked awestruck. Startled. And non-believing. All at the same time.

"Is that..." Carlos couldn't finish, hesitating and stumbling on the words he wanted to say but didn't know how to ask.

"Yes," I said firmly (far more evenly than I felt). "This is Britney. Our daughter."

Carlos flinched, opening and shutting his mouth a few times, but he was apparently too speechless by my admission to say anything sensible (entirely struck dumb, it would seem). I wasn't surprised. Annoyed. Slighted perhaps. But not alarmed. He had probably barely seen Britney since she was a baby or a very young toddler. I rather marvelled that Carlos remembered he even had a daughter, the way he'd behaved back then.

Suddenly another voice joined the chorus, one that told me everything was going to be alright (no matter how bad it had seemed beforehand).

"What is going on out here?" The voice questioned with undeniable authority.

It was Lucas…

◆ ◆ ◆ ◆ ◆ ◆ ◆

Ma insisted that I listened to everything Carlos had to say before making any rash decisions. And I confess that as I did so, he sounded truly remorseful as he dove into the tale of his past life. He left out crude points in the presence of young Britney, but all the adults in attendance quickly grasped his inferred meanings anyway. I got pretty wrapped up, hearing about his work, what made him start beating me, and what had eventually turned his life upside down – thinking he had killed his wife (when I hadn't got back up immediately, Carlos had irrationally feared the worst). I fidgeted and shifted so much, not meeting his eyes, that Britney felt compelled to sit on Lucas' lap instead of mine (which only made me feel even more panicky than ever). It felt like it left me more open somehow, more vulnerable to Carlos' close proximity. But I sensed Lucas also nearby, ready to step in at a moment's notice if necessary, and that gave me the patience to continue.

"And that's what led me here," Carlos finished. "I thought I recognised this place – bits and pieces returning to me from our earlier days here. Do you remember the log we used to sit on by the creek? Is it still there…?"

I squirmed uncomfortably under his direct gaze, but thankfully Ma quickly took over, so I didn't have to say anything in response. *Were they all expecting everything to go straight back to normal, just like that?* I had looked forward to this day (longed for it even), but now that it was actually here, I didn't think I was quite ready for things to change again so suddenly. Part of me just wanted to stay at the cottage with Ma and Britney. Not forever. Just long enough for me to accustom myself to the fact that my husband was back, pleading for another chance. I had every intention of doing so, but not just yet. I raised my chin and glared straight at Carlos to say so. To say "yes, given time you can have another chance. Yes, we can still be man and wife – I have forgiven you." But suddenly I caught the anxious look on his face and the words died on my lips. *Carlos had been hurt back then too!* In different ways perhaps, but I realised that he was also still recovering from his own trauma. *How had I not seen the depth of his pain and confusion earlier?* Carlos had been stuck in a rut – trapped. With no one to help him out of it. Every time Carlos had lashed out, he had simply been inflicting himself with more damage than I could ever have imagined! Something changed inside me. The gulf dividing us seemed to shorten, closing the very gap that had stood between us. It didn't vanish entirely, but substantially diminished, and somehow everything suddenly seemed to be in focus. More clear-cut. I still needed time to think, but now I knew what it was that I was grasping for – was there some way, any possible scenario, that would work? Anything that would let us heal, together…?

Chapter Twelve

Lucas hired Carlos to work in his carpentry business, giving him the perfect opportunity to prove to me how much Carlos had changed and that he deeply regretted what had been done. The empty shell of a man gradually got back to his usual carefree self, with Lucas and the other men in the village to offer guidance and better role models to follow than the detrimental ones Carlos had previously been exposed to at the dockyard.

I had plenty of time to observe his behaviour, and as more glimmers of his youthful character shone through (establishing himself to be the man I once loved), my decision was made. There was only one thing holding me back. One person standing in my way: Britney. *How would Britney feel if I were to move back in with Carlos?* It was clear that she hated having her pa constantly nearby, but then she didn't know the man as I had. Take away the drunken, abusive man, that image of him in her head, and Britney would have nothing there to fall back on. Certainly not in the way I could. Carlos had returned to the general figure of our happy childhood, but wasn't exactly the same. He was older now, and acted more mature than he had ever done back then. Although, perhaps a great deal of that had to do with Lucas' influence... Despite being an orphan from an extremely tender age, the younger man had an air of confidence and gentility around him (this, I found, was most meticulously learned under the late tutelage of Pa, and had been thoroughly ingrained within him. And I knew Pa would have been proud of his adoptive son). And son-in-law, who exhibited similar such traits as time wore on, seeking to mimic Lucas' kindly nature.

I sought after a moment when Carlos would be alone, knowing we needed to plan our future and figure out what to do with Britney's reticence. *Could we help her overcome such an awful history with Carlos? Or would she always hold such actions against him? Permanently...* We had so many things to discuss, so much to sort through, problems and shady areas that had to be cleared up before any of us could move on with our lives.

"I see why she'd be hesitant," Carlos frowned when we sat down together to discuss the issue. We had gone down to the creek again, as we'd always found it a private spot to clear the air when either one of us had something mildly unpleasant to say to the other. "I haven't exactly been the most ideal person to be her pa lately. But I do want to set that right, if I can."

"Perhaps she just needs more time to adjust." I encouraged. "Britney may take longer to come around than I did... Whatever can we do?"

"I've purchased a cottage," Carlos admitted. "On the other side of the village. Would you consider joining me there? Britney doesn't have to come – she could stay here, with your ma and Lucas, if she would prefer that."

"I don't know what she'd choose," I hesitated. "I hate to think that she might believe I was deserting her again..."

"You did what any mother should have done in your situation." Carlos put his arm on my shoulder. "I commend what you did – I do not deserve to have a daughter."

I spluttered. *That, coming from Carlos, who used to claim that he'd be the most terrific Pa ever!* But he was right… and had openly commented upon his many failings on that count.

"Nor do I," I agreed, unwilling to let him feel like he had been the only one to make mistakes. "She has turned out better than both of us!"

"We have your ma to thank for that." Carlos laughed (although it still had a hollow sort of ring to it).

"And Lucas," I added, smiling.

"Yes, and Lucas," Carlos' chuckle sounded more genuine this time. "Who would've thought that my golden-haired beauty would end up with such a dependable, patient little brother to make us see reason…"

◆ ◆ ◆ ◆ ◆ ◆ ◆

Britney appeared horrified when I asked her once again to reconsider her deep-rooted opinion of Carlos.

"You actually want to go back to him?" She squealed in surprise. "After everything you've been through to get away from it all!"

"He's not like that anymore, Britney," I tried to explain, but felt entirely inadequate to convey the right sentiments to her. It seemed as if I was being hemmed in against a brick wall by her startling amount of opposition (who knew she had such a fiery temper when roused!). "He got a dangerous job, and it led to all sorts of terrible things that Carlos should never have done. But it's all better, we've worked things out. I love who he is now, not because of how he might have lived before. He's the man I gave my heart to, Britney. Please? Just give us a chance – it'll be different this time. I promise…"

"No! I certainly shall not!" Britney quickly fired back, flouncing out of the room in response. "And you can think twice about moving in with that man, because I won't let you!"

So (with an attitude like that), I was rather surprised when she found Carlos and me hugging outside the cottage only a few days later and reacted in much the opposite way to whatever it was that I had expected. Britney pushed us apart! But it wasn't to break us up… it was more like she didn't want to be left out or excluded from such an important moment. Whisper ran in circles around us, as if guarding her newly acquired family. I breathed a deep sigh of relief, letting go of my cares, because this was how it should always have been – all three of us, united together for a better future.

Chapter Thirteen

It was difficult leaving Ma (she had become rather frail in old age), but Britney and I packed up our things and moved into the cottage Carlos had picked out especially for us. It was a beautiful place, and far better kept than the last one I had been required to look after. Carefully placed windows ensured a decent amount of light during the day and allowed many hours of sunshine to warm it through.

We often took meals over and ate with Ma and Lucas, as she was unable to get out and about as much as she used to. And we still helped out with extra chores whenever we could do so, to spare her from overexerting herself. But it wasn't the same as living under her roof. Even so, I enjoyed having my own kitchen again. And Carlos was delighted to return home each day to the sounds of our laughter (and the wonderful smells if ever Britney or I had spent the day baking!). And how I loved being able to invite my friends over to visit, welcoming them into my own home (Carlos had never allowed guests before). Britney was able to spend more time running and playing with the other children and it pleased me to see how happy and healthy she looked. My daughter could grow up the right way from now on – there was simply no more reason for her to have to behave like an adult far before her years demanded it.

Not many folks in the village asked much about what Carlos and I had done, or where we had gone (whether or not Ma had admonished them not to, as an upstanding member of the community, I never found out), but our complicated history was left exactly where it should have been – banished into the past. I didn't think it necessary to enlighten any of them either, and yet (for the most part), we were welcomed home with much generosity and good cheer.

I was grateful that Ma had taken thought and noted down the Cordwell's forwarding address, so while I could not see Monica face to face, we could still write to each other regularly and keep in touch. As soon as I had obtained enough stationery and appropriate ink from the store (and borrowed Ma's best quill!), I sat down to pen out a long letter. I could not include too many details of what had transpired between Carlos, Britney, and me or what we had been through. But I could update her on the more 'normal' pieces of interest, such as that we had moved back to our old village after many years of putting up elsewhere. I told Monica how sorry I was that she had gone before my return and how much I had missed our incessant talking on outings. I was surprised by how many pages filled so quickly – she would be overjoyed to receive such unexpected correspondence with the next post. I imagined her tearing the envelope open and eagerly scanning its contents before rushing to pen a reply. Monica had never been much of a writer and I was probably just as surprised to find an almost equally long letter waiting for me nearly one week later. She thanked me for mine, commenting briefly on some points, before going on with her own news. I was extremely pleased to learn that Monica had become a secretary (and writing short articles), for a local newspaper company. I chuckled with mirth reading what she had said about how much she enjoyed working there. Dynamic Monica, always on the go, settling down to work in an office (however large), seemed so contrary to what I had previously known of the woman. But her tone sounded rather cheerful about the position and so I was quite delighted for her. I didn't know how life could get any better than it was in that moment! But then, somehow, it did… And it came in the shape of a young woman named Maisie Copperley.

Chapter Fourteen

It was Lucas who first introduced us all to her. The bright-eyed, bubbly Maisie was someone he'd known as a child but hadn't seen for a long time (he had unexpectedly bumped into her in the village one day, just as she was arriving to visit some extended members of her family). Maisie was thrilled to see him, Lucas barely even recognising her for who she really was – one of his neighbours from growing up. A middle child of the family that had originally taken him in when he was first orphaned. But Lucas had chosen not to remain there, instead taking to the road (and incidentally, stumbling across Ma and Pa instead). Maisie chatted easily with everyone, lightly joining in with familiar activities with no awkwardness or reservations. She was much younger than I and her upbeat outlook had not yet been marred by a lifetime of scars (despite having lost several members of her family through disease and then an unexpected accident which had quickly turned fatal). I savoured her company – it had been so long since I'd had a real friend to walk alongside me. Maisie apologised unnecessarily for only being able to stay in the village for a couple of weeks while she checked in on her aunt, but I saw the way Lucas' eyes lit up whenever he saw her out and about (or inadvertently entered the same room as him) and wondered if it might turn out differently to what she said.

Lucas and Maisie had always got along extremely well apparently, and they immediately fell into the same friendly banter they'd had as children (just as if they had known each other for all of their adult lives, despite not having seen the other for years!). None of us were very surprised, therefore, when the budding relationship quickly turned into something more. The announcement of their engagement was readily welcomed by everyone concerned, and the wedding was anticipated with great eagerness. Lucas and Maisie waited just long enough for the rest of Maisie's family to come along, and the date was set. Everyone scrambled about to complete their set preparations in time and to get each and every last detail planned out and organised to the couple's satisfaction. Britney was so happy when she got asked to be a flower girl for the special occasion. Maisie's own sister was her maid of honour, but Lucas chose Carlos to be his best man at the service that day (the gesture meant that he greatly valued my husband's friendship of late, and really wanted to include us all in their happiness). I could not have appreciated it more.

◆ ◆ ◆ ◆ ◆ ◆ ◆

The chosen day arrived, dawning bright and sunny, with a clear blue sky stretching from one horizon to the other. I helped Britney put on her new frock and carefully braided her hair into a pretty bun, leaving a few tendrils free to curl around each side of her face. Quickly, I pulled on my own best dress and hurried her along to the village chapel to await the arrival of everyone else. I thought we had gone early, but the foyer was packed with guests and many of the pews had already been taken. I wasn't a bit worried though, as we'd reserved the front few rows for family members only. I left Britney with the bridal party once they'd come and escorted Ma to our designated seats (greeting numerous folks as they called out to us). Lucas was standing near the altar at the front of the chapel, a tense look of eager anticipation written on his face, with Carlos hovering nearby (appearing dutifully solemn).

There was a 'whoosh' of skirts and chairs creaked as the congregation stood, the triumphant piano music signalling the grand entrance of the bride escorted by her pa. Folks sufficiently 'oohed' and 'aahed' over Britney traipsing elegantly down the aisle, and gasped over how beautiful Maisie looked in her gorgeous silk gown of pure white. She had the most treasured smile on her lips and Lucas was thoroughly beaming. Actually, I think everyone was beaming. It was the most wonderful ceremony (followed by a relaxed afternoon tea in the crowded hall), that I had ever had the privilege of attending. I smiled, tears lining my eyes, as I felt the gentle kick of the baby boy shifting positions inside me. I was so filled with joy that I thought I might just as well burst – our little family was growing.

Acknowledgements

I am very grateful to all the staff at Austin Macauley Publishers who worked on the production of my book and who played a huge role in making this publication possible. It has been a pleasure to work with all of you.

I want to recognise those who helped incite confidence in my writing, planted seeds of inspiration, or provided additional value to my manuscript in any way and often spent their time journeying right alongside me down the new road, delving enthusiastically into the wonderful, creative world of making books for the enjoyment of others.

I would also like to thank each of my friends and family members who encouraged me to follow my dream of becoming an author. I could not have made it this far without all your support and positive feedback.

About the Author

Alison has been writing short stories to share with friends and family for many years and always enjoys exploring her creativity when putting pen to paper. She is excited to have the opportunity to share her love of writing with others.

Alison loves spending time with her pet dog, a Labrador x Huntaway, called Smoky, teaching her tricks and taking her for walks. She lives in a small town in New Zealand near many beautiful parks and beaches.

Alison has been playing trombone since about 2010 and euphonium since mid-2019 and always likes getting together with a few friends to 'make a joyful noise'. She also enjoys a bit of photography when she gets the chance, especially if it involves taking pictures of sunsets.